Two Times the Fun

BEVERLY CLEARY

Two Times the Fun

Illustrated by
Carol Thompson

HARPERCOLLINS*PUBLISHERS*

Library of Congress Cataloging-in-Publication Data
Cleary, Beverly.
    Two times the fun / Beverly Cleary ; illustrated by Carol Thompson.—1st ed.
        p.   cm.
    Summary: Jimmy and Janet, four-year-old twins, share the adventures of digging a hole to China, finding a worthy recipient for their dog biscuits, shopping for new shoes, and getting real beds to replace their cribs.
    ISBN 0-06-057921-8 — ISBN 0-06-057922-6 (lib. bdg.)
    [1. Twins—Fiction.   2. Brothers and sisters—Fiction.]   I. Thompson, Carol, 1973– ill.   II. Title.
PZ7.C5792Gt 2005   2004004118
[E]—dc22

First Edition
1 2 3 4 5 6 7 8 9 10

www.harperchildrens.com

To the original twins

Contents

·1·

The Real Hole

Jimmy and Janet are twins. They have the same mother, the same father, and the same birthday, too. Jimmy always has Janet to play with and Janet always has Jimmy to play with. Even though Jimmy and Janet are both four years old, they do not always like the same things.

Janet likes pretend things. She likes to pretend that a block is a cup of tea or that two paper bags are a pair of boots.

But Jimmy—Jimmy likes real things. He doesn't want to play with a toy hammer and toy nails. He wants to play with a real grown-up hammer and real grown-up nails. When Jimmy's father brings him a present, the first thing Jimmy asks is,

"Is it real?"

One morning Jimmy said to his father, "I want to dig a hole. I want to dig the biggest hole in the world."

"That's a good idea," said Jimmy's father, and he found a place in the corner of the backyard where Jimmy could dig a hole.

Jimmy took his toy shovel and began to dig. He put the shovel into the dirt and pushed it down with his foot, the way he had seen his father dig. When he tried to lift the dirt—*snap, crack*—the handle of his shovel broke.

"Daddy! My shovel broke," cried Jimmy. "I need a real shovel."

"The real shovel is too big," said Jimmy's father, "but you can try." He brought Jimmy the real shovel, which was much bigger than Jimmy. Jimmy worked and worked, but the real shovel was too big and heavy for him. The hole Jimmy was digging was hardly a hole at all.

"I have an idea," said Jimmy's father. He went into the garage and came out with a shovel that was just Jimmy's size. "I had forgotten we had this," he said.

"Is it real?" asked Jimmy.

"Yes, it's real," answered Jimmy's father. "This is the kind of shovel soldiers use to dig trenches. It is called a trench digger."

"Real soldiers?" asked Jimmy.

"Real soldiers," answered his father.

While Janet played in her swing, Jimmy began to dig. The real shovel that real soldiers used was just the right size for Jimmy. He could never break the handle of this shovel. No, sir!

He pushed the shovel into the ground, lifted out the dirt, and tossed it out of the hole. Push, lift, toss. This was the way Jimmy wanted to dig.

Then Jimmy went to the front yard so he could show his shovel to Mr. Lemon, the mailman, when he brought the mail.

"Say, that's a real shovel you have there!" said Mr. Lemon.

"Yup, I'm digging the biggest hole in the world," answered Jimmy, and he went back to digging in the backyard. Mr. Lemon liked his shovel!

"My, what a big hole," said Jimmy's mother, when she came outside to tell Jimmy and Janet that lunch was ready. Then she brushed the dirt off Jimmy's jeans and emptied the dirt out of Jimmy's shoes.

After lunch, while Janet galloped around on her hobbyhorse, Jimmy went right on digging. Push, lift, toss. The hole was almost up to his knees when his mother came outside, brushed the dirt off his jeans, emptied the dirt out of his shoes, and took him inside for his nap.

Jimmy was so tired from digging all morning that he took a good long nap. When he woke up he climbed out of his bed in a hurry, so he could go outside and dig in his hole some more.

But when Jimmy opened the back
door, he discovered that Janet was
already awake. She was not only awake,
she was out in the backyard sitting in
his hole! "That's my hole!" said Jimmy.

"I am a little bird sitting on a nest," said Janet.

"That is not a nest!" yelled Jimmy. "That is my hole, and I want to dig in it!"

"Children!" said the twins' mother. "Janet, let Jimmy have his hole. It's his, because he dug it."

"I just wanted to borrow Jimmy's hole for a little while," said Janet, as she climbed out and went to play on the slide.

"I don't want Janet to borrow my hole," said Jimmy, and he began to dig with his real shovel. He dug and dug. Push, lift, toss. The hole grew deeper and deeper. Pretty soon it was up to

Jimmy's knees. Still Jimmy dug. He had never worked so hard, but of course he had never had a real shovel to work with before. Then some dirt around the edge of the hole fell into the hole and buried Jimmy's shoes. Jimmy was not discouraged.

He pulled his feet out of the dirt, shoveled the dirt out of the hole, and went on digging. "Jimmy, you look so hot and tired," said his mother. "Why don't you rest awhile?"

"No," said Jimmy. "I'm digging the biggest hole in the world." Pretty soon Jimmy's mother and father came to look at the hole.

"My goodness," said his mother.

"What are you going to do with such a big hole?"

"We could pretend it is a place to catch fish," said Janet. "I could tie a string to a stick and pretend I am catching fish."

"No," said Jimmy. "It isn't a place to catch fish. It is a real big hole."

"What are you going to do with your real hole?" asked his father.

"We could pretend it is a place where baby rabbits live," said Janet. "I could get in the hole and pretend I am a baby rabbit."

"No!" said Jimmy. "It isn't a place where baby rabbits live. It is a real hole, and I made it with a real shovel."

Then Mrs. Robbins, the lady next door, came over to see Jimmy's hole. "My, what a big hole!" she said. "What are you going to do with such a great big hole?" Jimmy did not know what he was going to do with such a great big hole. Muffy, the dog that lived next door, came over and sniffed the hole.

"Muffy could bury bones in the hole," said Janet.

"No!" said Jimmy. "Muffy can dig his own hole."

Then the man who lived next door came to see Jimmy's hole. "Say, that is a big hole!" he said. "What are you going to do with such a great big hole?" Everybody thought Jimmy should do

something with his hole. Everybody
but Jimmy. He liked his hole just the
way it was.

"I am going to keep my hole," he said.

"I'm afraid not," said his father. "If
you or Janet ran across the yard and
fell into the hole, you might get hurt."
Jimmy looked at his father. Not keep

his real hole that he had dug with his real shovel?

"I want to keep my hole," he said.

"Now Jimmy," said his father. "I don't want you or Janet to get hurt."

"You said I could dig a big hole," Jimmy reminded him.

"Yes, but I didn't know you could dig such a big hole," answered his father. This made Jimmy feel better. His father hadn't known he could dig such a big hole.

"There must be something we could do with such a nice hole," said Jimmy's mother. "It's too bad not to use it for something, when Jimmy has worked so hard." So Jimmy and Janet and their mother and father thought and thought. What could they do with such a big hole?

"I know!" said Jimmy's father.

"What?" asked Jimmy and Janet.

"You wait and see. It's a surprise," answered their father, and he backed the car out of the garage and drove away.

"What do you suppose he's going to get?" asked the twins' mother.

"Is it a big water pipe?" asked Jimmy.

"Is it a family of baby rabbits?" asked Janet.

"I don't know," answered their mother. "We will have to wait and see."

After a while Jimmy and Janet's

father came back. When he got out
of the car he took something out of
the backseat. It was a tree growing in
a big tin can. "Is it a real tree?" asked
Jimmy.

"Yes, it's a real spruce tree," answered
his father, "and your hole is just the
right size to plant it in." Jimmy grabbed

his shovel. He wanted to help plant a real tree in his real hole.

His father took the tree out of the can and set it in the hole. With the hose they watered the roots of the tree. Then they filled in the hole with dirt.

"Now we have a real tree growing in our yard," said Jimmy's mother.

"We can pretend it's a Christmas tree," said Janet.

"It *is* a Christmas tree," said her father. "This year we can have two Christmas trees, one in the house and one in the yard."

"You didn't know I could dig a hole for a tree," said Jimmy, who was pleased with what he had done.

"No, we didn't," said Jimmy's mother. Then she brushed the dirt off Jimmy's jeans and emptied the dirt out of Jimmy's shoes.

"It was a real grown-up hole," Jimmy said proudly.

"Yes, sir!" said Jimmy's father. "A real grown-up hole!"

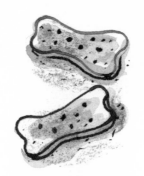

· 2 ·

Two Dog Biscuits

Jimmy and Janet do many things together. They draw pictures of funny bugs and birthday cakes and eggs in a nest.

They sing "Skip to My Lou." They pump themselves up high in their swings, and they swat flies.

Jimmy and Janet like being twins because they always have each other to play with.

They get up at the same time and go to bed at the same time.

Janet always has Jimmy to swing with her on the glider, and Jimmy

always has Janet to sit on the other
end of the teeter-totter.

"I think twins are a very nice
arrangement," said Mother.

"What does 'very nice arrangement'
mean?" asked Janet, who liked big
words.

"It means I'm glad I have twins,"
answered Mother. Jimmy and Janet
think twins are a nice arrangement, too.

One morning Jimmy and Janet went next door to see Mrs. Robbins and her dog, Muffy. When they came home Jimmy was carrying a dog biscuit shaped like a bone. Janet was carrying a dog biscuit shaped like a bone, too.

"See what Mrs. Robbins gave us," they said.

"see what Mrs. Robbins gave us."

"What are you going to do with two dog biscuits?" asked Mother.

"I'm going to keep my dog biscuit," said Jimmy.

"I'm going to keep my dog biscuit, too," said Janet. "It is a nice little dog biscuit."

"All right," said Mother, "but be sure you don't eat the dog biscuits. Dog biscuits are for dogs."

Janet laid her dog biscuit on a chair. Jimmy laid his dog biscuit on the couch. When Mother started to sit on the couch, she asked, "Whose dog biscuit is this?"

"My dog biscuit," answered Jimmy, and put his dog biscuit on the kitchen table.

Janet put her dog biscuit on the kitchen table, too. She did not want Mother to sit on her dog biscuit.

At lunchtime Mother said, "Put your dog biscuits away, children. I don't want you to get mixed up and eat them for lunch. Dog biscuits are for dogs."

Jimmy and Janet put their dog biscuits in their pockets.

After lunch and naps Mother said, "It's time for some clean clothes." When Jimmy took off his jeans, his dog biscuit fell out of his pocket. When Janet took off her overalls, her dog biscuit fell out of her pocket, too.

"My goodness," said Mother. "Every place I look I see dog biscuits. Why don't you take the dog biscuits next door and give them to Muffy?"

"Muffy has dog biscuits," said Janet. "He has a big bag of them."

"Then give the dog biscuits to some other dog," said Mother.

"Dogs don't come to our house," said Jimmy.

"Then let's go find a dog," said Mother. "Put on your clean clothes, and we'll go for a walk and find a dog that would like two dog biscuits."

So Jimmy and Janet, wearing their clean clothes, went for a walk with Mother. "Be on the lookout for a dog," said Mother.

"What does 'be on the lookout' mean?" asked Janet.

"It means to watch for something," answered Mother. Jimmy and Janet and Mother were on the lookout for a dog.

The first dog they met was a big brown dog. "I don't want to give my dog biscuit to a brown dog," said Jimmy.

growl

grrrr

grrrr

"I don't want to give my dog biscuit to a big dog," said Janet.

"Oh, dear," said Mother. "I guess we will have to find another dog."

After a while they met a small white dog. "I'm sure this dog is very hungry," said Mother. The little dog barked. *Yip-yip-yip.*

"No," said Janet. "That is not a nice dog. I want to give my nice little dog  biscuit to a nice little dog."

"Oh, dear," said Mother. "I guess we will have to find another dog."

Then they saw Mr. Lemon delivering mail across the street.

"Mr. Lemon!" Jimmy shouted. "We have two dog biscuits!"

Janet called out, "We're going to give them to a nice dog!"

"Lucky dog!" Mr. Lemon called back.

After a while they met a big black dog. "I'm sure this dog would like two dog biscuits," said Mother.

The dog was hungry. He barked. *Woof-woof-woof.*

Woof!

"No," said Jimmy. "I don't like dogs that bark."

"Oh, dear," said Mother. "I guess we will have to find another dog."

They went on walking. They met big dogs, little dogs, smooth dogs, curly

dogs, dogs that sniffed, and dogs that wagged their tails. Each time they met a dog Jimmy and Janet said, "No, I don't want to give my dog biscuit to *this* dog."

"Oh, dear, such picky children!" said Mother. "It's almost time for Daddy to come home, and we have not found the right dog to give the dog biscuits to. What are we going to do?"

Jimmy and Janet thought and thought. What were they going to do? They did not really want to give their dog biscuits to a dog. If Muffy had his own dog biscuits, other dogs must have dog biscuits, too.

"We could give the dog biscuits to a cat," said Janet and laughed. What a funny idea, dog biscuits for a cat!

"Oh, no," said Mother. "A cat couldn't eat a dog biscuit, because it would be too hard for his teeth. Dog biscuits are for dogs." Just the same, on the way home Jimmy and Janet were on the lookout for a cat.

When they were almost home Janet spied a big tiger cat snoozing on a driveway in the sunshine. "There is a cat," she said. "I'm going to give him my dog biscuit."

"I'm afraid that cat does not want your dog biscuit," said Mother.

Janet tiptoed over to the cat and laid her dog biscuit under his nose. "Here is a present for you, kitty," she said.

The cat opened one eye. He opened the other eye. He stood

up and stretched. He sniffed the dog biscuit.

Then he sat down and began to eat. It was hard work for him to eat such a hard biscuit, but he crunched and  munched and pretty soon the biscuit was gone. The cat licked his whiskers, looked around, and said, "Meow."

"He liked my dog biscuit," said Janet. "He's saying thank you."

"He wants another dog biscuit," said Jimmy. "Here, kitty. Here is another present for you." The cat crunched and munched Jimmy's dog biscuit,

and when it was all
gone he sat up and
began to wash.

"You didn't know
a cat would eat dog
biscuits," Jimmy said
to Mother. "You said dog biscuits were
for dogs." He and Janet laughed. What
fun it was to know something a grown-
up didn't know!

"No, I didn't know a cat would eat dog
biscuits, but now
I know it," said
Mother, and
she laughed,
too. "Oh,
look, there's

Daddy coming home from work."

"Daddy! Daddy!" shouted Janet, running down the sidewalk to meet him. "We gave our dog biscuits to a cat and he ate them!"

"Daddy! Daddy!" shouted Jimmy, running down the sidewalk to meet him. "Mother said the cat wouldn't eat the dog biscuits, but he did! She didn't know!"

Daddy caught Jimmy and Janet and picked them both up at the same time. "Your mother didn't know a cat would eat dog biscuits!" he exclaimed. "What a big joke on Mother!"

·3·

The Growing-Up Feet

"When are my feet going to grow up?" Jimmy asked one morning as he wiggled his toes.

"They're growing all the time," said Mother. "They have grown so much that it is time to go to the shoe store and talk to Mr. Markle about new shoes."

Bargains inside!

Shoe Store

½ Price

Sale! today

"For me, too?" asked Janet, Jimmy's twin sister.

"For both of you," said Mother.

"Our feet are growing up!" shouted Jimmy. "Our feet are growing up!"

"New shoes, new shoes, we're going to get new shoes!" sang Janet. Then she said, "And I'm going to surprise Mr. Lemon with new shoes when he brings the mail." Janet liked to surprise people, especially Mr. Lemon.

Mother and the twins drove to the shoe store, where they sat in three chairs in a row, with Mother in the middle.

Mr. Markle pulled up a stool and

sat down in front of them. "What will my favorite customers have today?" he asked.

"Shoes," said Jimmy. "Our feet are growing up."

"No kidding," said Mr. Markle. He felt the toes of Jimmy's and Janet's shoes. Then he took off their shoes and asked each of them to stand on his measuring stick while he slid the wooden piece to the tips of their toes.

Mr. Markle shook his head. "Sorry," he said. "You kids aren't ready for new shoes."

No new shoes! Jimmy and Janet looked at Mother and said, "You told us we were ready for new shoes."

Mother sighed. "Mothers can be wrong sometimes," she said. That made Jimmy and Janet feel better—a little, but not much.

Mr. Markle looked disappointed, too. He sniffed and rubbed his eyes with his fists and looked so silly that Jimmy and Janet almost smiled.

Janet leaned against Mother. "I won't have a surprise for Mr. Lemon today," she said and looked very, very sad. "Mr. Lemon likes me to surprise him."

"We'll think of another surprise," said Mother.

"But it won't be new shoes," said Janet.

"I *want* new shoes," said Jimmy.

"Now, Jimmy," said Mother. "You're a big boy."

"No, I'm not!" said Jimmy. "My feet didn't grow up."

"How would you each like a balloon?" asked Mr. Markle.

Jimmy and Janet took the balloons, but they did not really want balloons. They wanted new shoes.

"You know something?" said Mr. Markle. "We have some boots on sale."

"We can't buy boots to fit old shoes," said Mother.

"These boots stretch," said Mr. Markle. "They will fit old shoes and new shoes, too. And you know something else? These boots are red."

Red boots. Jimmy and Janet looked up at Mother.

"Good," said Mother. "Let's buy new boots."

"For me?" asked Jimmy.

"For me?" asked Janet.

"For both of you," said Mother.

Mr. Markle brought out bright red boots, which fit the old shoes. "There you are, kids," he said. "Just what the Easter Bunny ordered."

Jimmy and Janet thought Mr. Markle was such a silly man. They knew Easter was a long time ago.

Jimmy wore his boots, but Janet carried hers in their box. The twins were so happy they didn't even stop to pet the hobbyhorse on their way out the door. Mother remembered to say "Thank you" to Mr. Markle.

When Mother and the twins returned home, they found Mr. Lemon had already delivered the mail. Janet hid her box of boots in the closet. "I'm going to save my boots to show Daddy," she said, "and tomorrow I will surprise Mr. Lemon."

"Jimmy, don't you want to take off

your boots?" asked Mother.

"No," said Jimmy and ran out into the yard. In a little while he came back. "I can't find any puddles," he said.

"Of course there aren't any puddles," said Mother. "It isn't raining."

"When is it going to rain?" asked Jimmy.

"I don't know," answered Mother. "There aren't any clouds, so it won't rain today."

"Will it rain tomorrow?" asked Jimmy.

"I don't know," said Mother. "I don't think so."

"The next day?" asked Jimmy.

"I don't know." Mother sounded tired as she made sandwiches for lunch.

New boots and no puddles. Jimmy pretended he was walking in puddles, but he wanted *real* puddles with *real* water. Janet waited and waited for Daddy to come home so she could show him her red boots in their box.

When Daddy came home he was surprised once to see Jimmy wearing new boots and surprised twice when Janet opened her box to show him her boots. After the surprise, Janet put her boots on, too.

"Our feet didn't grow up," said Jimmy, "and Mother said they did."

"Don't worry. They will," said Daddy.

Jimmy and Janet wore their boots while they ate their dinner. Their feet were hot, but they didn't care. At bedtime they pulled their boots on over the feet of their sleepers.

When Mother said they could not sleep with boots over their sleepers because their feet would be too hot,

they slept with their boots on their hands.

In the morning Jimmy and Janet pulled their new boots on over their old shoes. "My goodness," said Mother. "You will wear your boots out before we have any rain."

This morning Daddy put on an old pair of pants and a sweatshirt.

"Are you going to stay home today?" asked Jimmy as he watched Daddy shave. He liked to watch so he would know how when he was old enough to shave off whiskers of his own.

"Yes. Today is Saturday," answered Daddy.

Janet, who knew she would never

have whiskers like Daddy, was in the kitchen with Mother. "I wish Mr. Lemon would hurry up and come," she said.

After breakfast Jimmy said to Daddy, "If we went for a walk, maybe we could find some puddles."

Daddy smiled. "I'm afraid not, but I know what we can do. Come outside with me."

"I'm going to sit on the front step and watch for Mr. Lemon," said Janet.

Daddy backed the car out of the garage. Then he turned on the hose and started to wash the car. Water ran down the driveway. "Puddles!" shouted Jimmy and began to splash. Janet decided Mr. Lemon would be surprised to see wet boots when the sun was shining, so she splashed, too.

Mother stood in the doorway watching her twins have fun. Daddy turned the hose on the grass and made a big puddle. Jimmy and Janet squished and splashed in the wet grass. Their boots were wet, but their shoes were dry.

Janet was sitting near mother when they saw Mr. Lemon coming down the street with his leather bag full of letters and catalogs. "You stay here," Janet told Jimmy. "I want to surprise Mr. Lemon."

"Okay," said Jimmy. He went on stomping and splashing.

"Say!" said Mr. Lemon when Janet ran to meet him. "Look at those red boots and all those wet footprints when the sun is shining." Janet was happy because she could see Mr. Lemon was really surprised.

When the mailman reached their house, Jimmy stopped splashing to explain, "My feet didn't grow up. They are still the same size inside my boots."

"Don't worry," said Mr. Lemon. "Before you know it, your feet will be bigger than mine."

"They will?" Jimmy looked

at Mr. Lemon's feet. They were even bigger than Daddy's feet.

"And do you know something?" asked Mr. Lemon as he handed Jimmy the catalogs to carry. "When you get new shoes, those boots will grow to fit."

Now it was Janet's turn to be surprised. "How did you know?" she asked Mr. Lemon.

"I've learned a thing or two in my lifetime," said Mr. Lemon.

Jimmy and Janet splashed in their puddle. "We have growing-up feet!" they shouted. "We have growing-up boots, too!"

Mr. Lemon said so, and he knew a thing or two.

•4•

Janet's Thingamajigs

"I can't find the thingamajigs," Mother said when Jimmy fell down and skinned his knee. "What happened to the thingamajigs?"

Thingamajigs was a word Mother sometimes used when she was excited or in a hurry. Janet enjoyed finding out what thingamajigs meant each time her

mother used the word. This time it meant Band-Aids.

While Mother took care of Jimmy's knee, Janet found a red plastic paper clip, a little wheel, and a shiny bead. They were just right to hold in her hand. "Are these thingamajigs?" she asked.

Mother laughed and said, "Yes, you could call those thingamajigs."

Janet carried her things around all morning. She showed them to Mr. Lemon when he brought the mail. "See my thingamajigs," she said.

"Well, what do you know? Thinga-majigs!" Mr. Lemon sounded surprised.

At lunchtime, Janet laid her plastic paper clip, her little wheel, and her shiny bead on a chair in the living room and said, "I don't want Jimmy to touch these things."

"They're just old stuff," said Jimmy, who wanted very much to touch them, so he did. He touched them every time Janet wasn't looking. He liked to hold them, too.

He touched them until Janet caught him at it and said, "Jimmy, those are my thingamajigs."

"No," said Jimmy, holding on to them.

"Mother, Jimmy won't give me my thingamajigs," said Janet, "and I asked him in a nice, polite voice."

"I'm not hurting them," said Jimmy, who could be stubborn.

"Jimmy, give me my thingamajigs!"

yelled Janet. Her voice was not polite at all.

"No," said Jimmy and turned his back.

Janet pushed Jimmy.

Jimmy yelled, "Janet is pushing me!" Then he pushed Janet.

"Children!" cried Mother as she came out of the kitchen. "Stop this at once. Jimmy, give Janet her little things. You can find toys of your own."

"Janet is pushing me!"

Jimmy threw Janet's things on the floor. "I

don't want other toys!" he shouted.

Janet picked up her things and put them back on the chair. "I don't want Jimmy to touch my thingamajigs," she said.

Mother said, "Janet, you cannot leave them on that chair. When Daddy comes home, he wants to sit on the chair. He doesn't want to sit on your toys. If you don't want Jimmy to touch your things, you should put them away."

So Janet found a paper bag in the kitchen. She put the red plastic paper clip, the little wheel, and the shiny bead into the bag, wrapped a rubber band around the top, and put it on her little bed. "Now Jimmy can't touch my thingamajigs," she said.

"I don't want to touch Janet's things," said Jimmy, but he *did* want to touch them, more than anything.

The next day, Janet found a spool, a doll's shoe, and a smooth green stone. She carried her new little things around while Jimmy pretended to put air in the tires of his dump truck. She showed them to Mr. Lemon who was surprised all over again. Then she laid her little things on a

chair and went
into Mother and
Daddy's room to
help Mother make
the big bed.
When she came
back, Jimmy
was not playing
with his dump
truck. He was holding her spool, her
doll's shoe, and her smooth green
stone.

"Jimmy is touching my thingamajigs!" Janet cried. "He took them
from the blue chair!"

"Children, I am at my wit's end,"
said Mother.

"What does 'at my wit's end' mean?"
asked Janet.

"It means I don't know what to do,"
answered Mother. "Jimmy, give Janet
her things."

Jimmy threw the toys on the floor. "I
am too big for those things," he said.
"They're just junk."

"They are not junk," said Janet. "They are my treasures."

Jimmy only pretended to play with his dump truck while she picked up her treasures and laid them on the blue chair again.

"Janet," said Mother, "you cannot leave your things on the blue chair. I do not want to sit on your toys. I told you if you don't want Jimmy to touch them, you should put them away."

"I am at my wit's end," said Janet. Then she found another paper bag in the kitchen. She put her spool, her doll's shoe, and her smooth green stone into her paper bag. She put a rubber band around the top of the bag and put it on her little bed. "Now Jimmy can't touch my thingamajigs," she said.

The next day the same thing happened with a feather, a piece of pink yarn, and an old lipstick case. And the day after that the same thing happened with a little stick, a pretty leaf, and an empty snail shell. Every day Janet found little things, and every day she put them into paper bags on her bed, where Jimmy could not touch them.

One day Mother said, "Janet, your bed is full of paper bags. When you go to sleep, you rustle like a mouse in a wastepaper basket. Don't you want to share some of your paper bags with Jimmy?"

"No," said Janet as she climbed over the rail of her little bed. "These are my paper bags."

"Oh, dear, what are we going to do?" asked Mother. "Janet's bed is so full of paper bags she rustles like a mouse in a wastepaper basket. There is scarcely room for her to sleep. What are we going to do?"

"Paper bags are silly," said Jimmy as he climbed over the rail of his bed. Neither twin would let Mother remove the sides of the little beds. Climbing over the rail was fun.

"Paper bags are not silly," said Janet. "Paper bags are nice."

"But, Janet, you have too many," said

Mother. "We will have to find another place for all your paper bags."

"I like being a mouse in a wastepaper basket," said Janet, and she went right on finding little things and putting them in paper bags on her bed. Every night she said, "*Squeak-squeak. I am a little mouse.*"

"*Grr-grr.* I am a fierce bear," said Jimmy. He did not sound like a fierce bear. He sounded like a cross boy.

Then one morning Mother said, "Today we are going to have a surprise."

"Is it strawberries?" asked Jimmy.

"Is it a nice soft kitten?" asked Janet.

"No, it isn't strawberries or a nice soft kitten," answered Mother. "You wait and see."

Jimmy and Janet thought and thought, but they could not think what Mother's surprise could be.

"If you watch out the front window, you will see it sometime this morning," said Mother.

Jimmy and Janet watched out the

front window. "When is it going to come? When is it going to come?" they asked over and over. They saw a boy riding a bicycle, a girl skipping rope, and a lady carrying a shopping bag. They saw cars, a tow truck, and a school bus, but they did not see a surprise. After a while they grew tired of watching and turned their little table upside down and pretended it was a boat.

And then, when the twins happened to look out the window, a big delivery truck came slowly down the street, paused, and turned into the driveway—Jimmy and Janet's driveway. Two men got out of the truck. They opened the back, lifted something out, and set it on the grass. It was a bed.

They lifted out another bed and set it on the grass, too. Grown-up beds!

"Beds!" shouted Jimmy and Janet. "Mother, are these beds for us?"

"Yes," answered Mother. "You are growing up. It is time for you to have big beds."

The men carried one bed into the house and set it on Janet's side of the bedroom. They carried the other bed into the house and set it on Jimmy's

side of the room. "There you are, kids," one of them said. "Sleep tight, and don't let the bedbugs bite."

Jimmy and Janet bounced up and down on their new grown-up beds while Mother stood in the hall and watched.

"What—will—you—do—with—our—little—beds?" Janet asked Mother as she bounced.

"Maybe we could have a garage sale," Mother answered. "Or send them to Goodwill."

Then Jimmy stopped bouncing. "What is Janet going to do with her paper bags?" he asked. "They will fall off her bed."

Janet stopped bouncing. She took her

paper bags from her old little bed and piled them on her new grown-up bed. When she climbed back on her bed, paper bags slid off all over the floor.

"Ha-ha," said Jimmy.

"Jimmy can have my old paper bags," said Janet. "I am not a mouse. I am a big girl, and I sleep in a big bed."

"I don't want Janet's paper bags," said Jimmy. "I am too big to play with little junk."

"So am I," said Janet.

The twins began to bounce again. "We are big! We are big!" they sang while Mother tried to gather up all of Janet's paper bags.

Then Jimmy and Janet heard Mr. Lemon poking letters and catalogs through the slot in the front door. They jumped off their beds and ran to meet him. "Mr. Lemon! Mr. Lemon!" they shouted when they opened the door. "We have big beds! We have big beds!"

"Wow! Big beds!" said Mr. Lemon. Jimmy and Janet could tell he was really surprised.

"Say, you are growing up!" said Mr. Lemon. "I never would have guessed."

Growing-up—that was what Jimmy and Janet wanted more than anything in the whole world. "We're growing up!" they shouted. "We're growing up!" Mr. Lemon said so and he had learned a thing or two in his lifetime.

BEVERLY CLEARY

is one of America's most popular authors. Born in McMinnville, Oregon, she lived on a farm in Yamhill until she was six and then moved to Portland. After college, she became a children's librarian in Yakima, Washington. In 1940, she married Clarence T. Cleary, and they became the parents of twins, now grown.

Mrs. Cleary's books have earned her many prestigious awards, including the American Library Association's Laura Ingalls Wilder Award, presented in recognition of her lasting contributions to children's literature. She has also received the 2003 National Medal of Arts from the National Endowment for the

Arts. Her *Dear Mr. Henshaw* was awarded the 1984 John Newbery Medal, and her *Ramona and Her Father* and *Ramona Quimby, Age 8* have been named Newbery Honor Books. In addition, her books have won more than thirty-five statewide awards based on the votes of her young readers. Her characters, including Henry Huggins, Ellen Tebbits, Otis Spofford, and Beezus and Ramona Quimby, as well as Ribsy, Socks, and Ralph S. Mouse, have delighted children for generations.

Visit Beverly Cleary on the World Wide Web at **www.beverlycleary.com**

Also by Beverly Cleary